W9-CIO-114

Help! Fire!

Dedicated to Paul Magnusson,
my "loves me no matter what" brother, from Graci.
Thanks for the memories.

HELP! FIRE!
© 1992 by A Corner of the Heart

Published by Multnomah Press Books
P.O. Box 1720
Sisters, OR 97759

Printed in the United States of America.

Questar Publishers, Inc.
Post Office Box 1720
Sisters, Oregon 97759

Help! Fire!

ESCAPING WITH MY LIFE

BY DORIS SANFORD
ILLUSTRATIONS BY GRACI EVANS

MULTNOMAH PRESS

Daniel didn't object to staying home. That was no problem—but he did miss seeing his friends at school. In this family, staying home sick meant staying in bed or on the couch all day and drinking orange juice. A guy could watch cartoons only so long before he wanted a little more action!

Fortunately, Daniel's mother ran a day-care center at home and soon there would be six babies and toddlers invading the house. He was propped up on the couch waiting.

Daniel had been sick before. Not like this, but *really* sick. He had been born with only half a spine and with both legs paralyzed. When he was six years old he had a major operation to remove both legs below his knees and to build a new backbone. The doctors said he could get around better without his legs. Daniel figured that if his legs didn't work, he didn't need them! Someday he might have artificial legs, but they would be "just for looks." He would never be able to walk.

The operation lasted nine hours. Daniel was only the second person in the world to have this surgery. He said he would just as soon *not* be famous for having an operation!

While in the hospital, Daniel met other kids who had disabilities as serious as his. Unlike many of them, he had never been able to walk, so he didn't feel disabled. He had never known anything different. Besides, there were too many fun things to think about other than wishing he could walk. One of those things was what he could do to make his roommates at the hospital laugh. He was pretty good at that.

Daniel was in the hospital for two weeks. When the doctor came to tell him he could go home, Daniel threw his arms around the doctor's neck, hugged him and said, "Thank you, thank you for helping me." The doctor said that after causing him so much pain, he'd almost rather Daniel had punched him in the nose!

Daniel wore a body cast for one year. But having a cast didn't stop him from doing the things he liked.

He still went fishing with his dad and two brothers. He still had pillow fights with his friends. He even went roller skating. Well, almost. His dad pulled him around in a wagon while everybody else skated.

At the end of the year, Daniel was out of the cast. It felt good. Daniel preferred to get around under his own power. Using his elbows to propel himself, he scooted anywhere he wanted to go. His arms were strong. He could swim almost as well as his brothers. Swimming, eating, and riding his hand-controlled bike were his favorite things to do.

Daniel could do most things boys his age did. Once his family took him snow skiing. Now, *that* was an adventure! He rode the ski lift to the top of the mountain and came down with a sled and poles.

Sometimes Daniel wrestled with his two older brothers. When the going got tough, he simply sat on their faces. "A guy's got to do what a guy's got to do," he said.

But today Daniel was home sick. Staying home because of a cold meant being bored. At least that is the way it had always been in the past. Daniel had no idea that this would be a day that he would never, never forget. It was the day he would become a hero!

At about eight o'clock that morning his older brother, Alan, and his mother looked out of the front window to see a young child running hard, then slip and fall. He was screaming and both of his knees were bloody. Mom glanced quickly at Daniel and said that she and Alan would be right back. They knew Eric, who lived only six blocks away. Alan held him and Mom drove him home.

When they arrived, they handed Eric over to his mom and stayed for about fifteen minutes until he was quiet and bandaged. They explained how he had been hurt.

As they turned to leave, Alan and his mom heard sirens—lots of them. The sounds were coming closer, louder and louder. Suddenly their faces turned white as they ran toward the car. It couldn't be . . . no please . . . not Daniel!

Daniel was alone in the house watching cartoons. He had snuggled under the blankets and enjoyed the warmth from the nearby wood stove.

Suddenly the kindling box next to the wood stove burst into flames. One minute he had been sleepy, cozy, and relaxed. Now, his heart was pounding so hard he thought it would pop right out of his chest. He could yell, but would anyone hear him? He'd have to put out the fire himself.

Daniel fell to the floor and pulled himself on his elbows to the blazing box of wood, dragging his blanket and pillows with him. He threw the pillows at the fire and they immediately burst into flames, too. Now the drapes and wallpaper were on fire. He hit the flames with his blanket, but it only seemed to fan them and make the fire burn more intensely.

He couldn't stand the heat. If he stayed much longer, he knew he would be burned. Sweat was pouring off his face. "Help me, somebody help me!" he yelled.

Daniel scooted on his elbows toward the front door. Maybe somebody would be on the sidewalk and would hear him. "Fire! Fire!" he called at the top of his voice.

No response.

He knew it was hopeless. No one could hear him. He couldn't get out. The doorknob was too high and he couldn't reach it. There was no way for him to open the front door.

His two dogs, Charlie and Shadow, stayed beside him. They felt responsible for their friend. The room was filling with smoke. Daniel began coughing and gasping for air.

Then he had an idea—he'd phone for help, that's what he'd do! He scooted toward the phone. It was up on the table, so he pulled the cord until the phone fell to the floor. When it fell, he punched the next-door neighbor's number. He knew the Carsons' number by heart. Good thing! The phone rang and rang. *Come on somebody, answer the phone! Please answer the phone! I'm going to die in this fire! The house will burn up,* his mind raced as the phone kept ringing. No one answered.

Then he remembered. He should call the emergency number, 911! It rang two times before someone answered. Daniel yelled into the receiver, "I'm nine years old and I don't have any legs. My house is on fire! Nobody is here but me and my dogs."

The dispatcher asked calmly, "Where do you live?" Daniel told him. Then the man said, "Go outside; we'll be there very soon." It had been more than Daniel could stand and he yelled, "I'm scared! I'm so scared! I can't get out. Help me!"

The dispatcher interrupted. "You need to try to get out. Which door would be easiest for you to get out?"

Daniel said, "Maybe, maybe I can push open the sliding glass door to the patio. I'll try."

The dispatcher told him to leave the phone off the hook. Daniel did and started toward the glass door. If only he could pull himself up into his wheelchair, but it was too far away from him. There was so much smoke now he could hardly see. The flames were right behind him.

He knew he could not reach the latch. He would have to jump from the floor with his hands and knock the latch open. It was a long way up to the latch, but he jumped. He couldn't reach it. He jumped again and again and again. Finally he pushed the lever up, and the door unlocked. Now to push it open!

The dogs moved ahead of him and as they bumped against the door, it opened just a crack. He slid his fingers into the opening and it moved. They all tumbled outside.

Daniel slid the heavy door shut and started to cry. Charlie and Shadow hovered, one dog on each side of him, taking turns licking his tears. Whatever happened, these dogs were not leaving Daniel. It was cold outside on this early January morning, but the dogs' fur "blankets" helped keep him warm. For a minute he chuckled. He felt like a hot-dog sandwich!

Daniel's heart was racing. He had never been more frightened. He yelled, "Please, someone come and help me!" The handle on the fence gate was too high for him to reach. No amount of jumping would allow him to move it. Maybe he could dig out underneath the patio fence. He didn't know how long that would take. He did know there wasn't much time left. Maybe if the dogs barked, someone would check to see if there was a problem. Why did they always bark when they weren't supposed to and keep quiet now?

The fire was spreading rapidly. It wouldn't be long before it reached the outside wall of the house. Daniel knew they were not safe yet.

A few blocks away Daniel's mom jumped into the car and Alan yelled, "Floor it!" As they got closer to their house, they saw fire trucks, four police cars, the sheriff's car, an ambulance, and a paramedic truck. They prayed, "Don't let it be Daniel!" They drove as quickly as they could and when they turned the last corner, they saw smoke billowing out of their house.

Daniel was locked inside!

The car had hardly stopped before Alan ran into the house and grabbed the fire extinguisher from the kitchen. He pointed the nozzle and sprayed while he called, "Daniel . . . it's okay . . . I'm here . . . hang in there, little buddy!" Then louder, "Daniel, where are you?"

A fireman grabbed Alan's jacket and pulled him outside. "It's okay, son; we can handle it. You stay outside. We'll find him." Alan left only because he didn't have a choice. He would wait outside with his mother.

The next thing Daniel knew, two firemen were looking over the top of the patio fence. Both dogs growled, and Daniel knew they meant to protect him from these intruders with the weird masks. He would have to tell them it was safe now, so they would allow the firemen to enter. "Thanks, you two mutts, but these are definitely the *good* guys!"

The firemen came in, picked up Daniel, and brought him to his mother. Charlie and Shadow followed, somehow aware that the worst was over and that they had done a good job of taking care of their master.

Daniel's teeth were chattering. His mom was crying, and Alan was so relieved that he joked to break the tension. "Hey, big guy, did you get bored and try to stir up some excitement?" But Daniel was too exhausted to respond.

Then his dad arrived. Daniel cried again when he saw him, saying, "I didn't make it happen, Dad." His dad leaned down close to his face and said, "I know, Son, it wasn't your fault. None of this was anybody's fault. It just happened. I love you and I'm *so* glad you are okay."

The neighbors gathered around the house. This was more excitement than they had seen in a long time. There were smiles and waves as Daniel was placed on the stretcher to leave with the paramedics for the hospital.

Alan sat quietly on a corner of the front lawn with the dogs. This had been a close call. He could have lost his little brother. Charlie and Shadow seemed to hear his thoughts and licked his face as if to say, "We took care of him."

The doctors at the hospital listened to Daniel's lungs and gave him some oxygen before they sent him back home.

Much of the house had burned. Black soot, ashes, and water were everywhere. The family would have to stay with friends until the house was repaired. As they were gathering their things together, the TV cameramen arrived along with the reporters. They wanted to talk to Daniel. The story would be on the evening news and in all the morning newspapers.

The next day Daniel was back at school. He rode a
school bus with a special lift for his wheelchair. In the
classroom his desk had been specially made for him so
he could easily move from his wheelchair to his desk.
Everyone in his classroom had brought a copy of the
morning newspaper with the story about Daniel. They
all wanted to know how he jumped to get the patio door
open, so Daniel jumped up on one hand and did a flip.
They got the picture!

His teacher smiled and leaned over to talk to another teacher standing beside him. "Someone special lives in that little body," she said. "Someone very special."

Discussion Questions

1. Daniel had his legs removed in an operation. Can you name three other kinds of disabilities?

2. How could you be a friend to a person who could not walk?

3. Daniel enjoyed many fun activities. His disability didn't stop him. Can you name some of the activities Daniel enjoyed?

4. How would you have felt if you had been in Daniel's situation when the fire started?

5. What is the first thing you should do if you are alone and a fire begins?

6. Daniel jumped from the floor to open the sliding door. Have you ever had to do something really hard? Tell about it.

7. Daniel's dogs were special friends. If you have a pet, tell why your pet is a special friend to you.